This Rising Moon book belongs to

______________________________

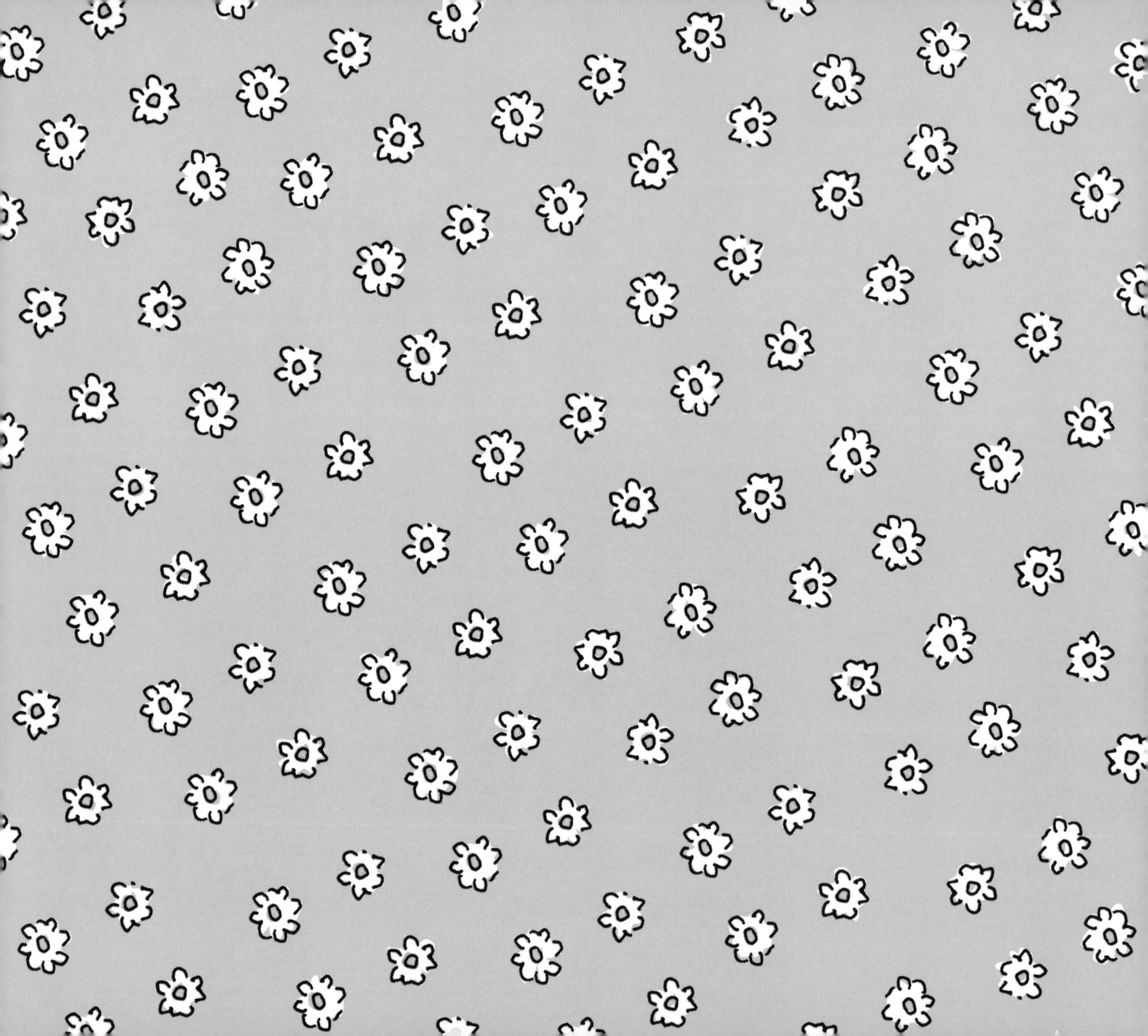

# Do Princesses Wear Hiking Boots?

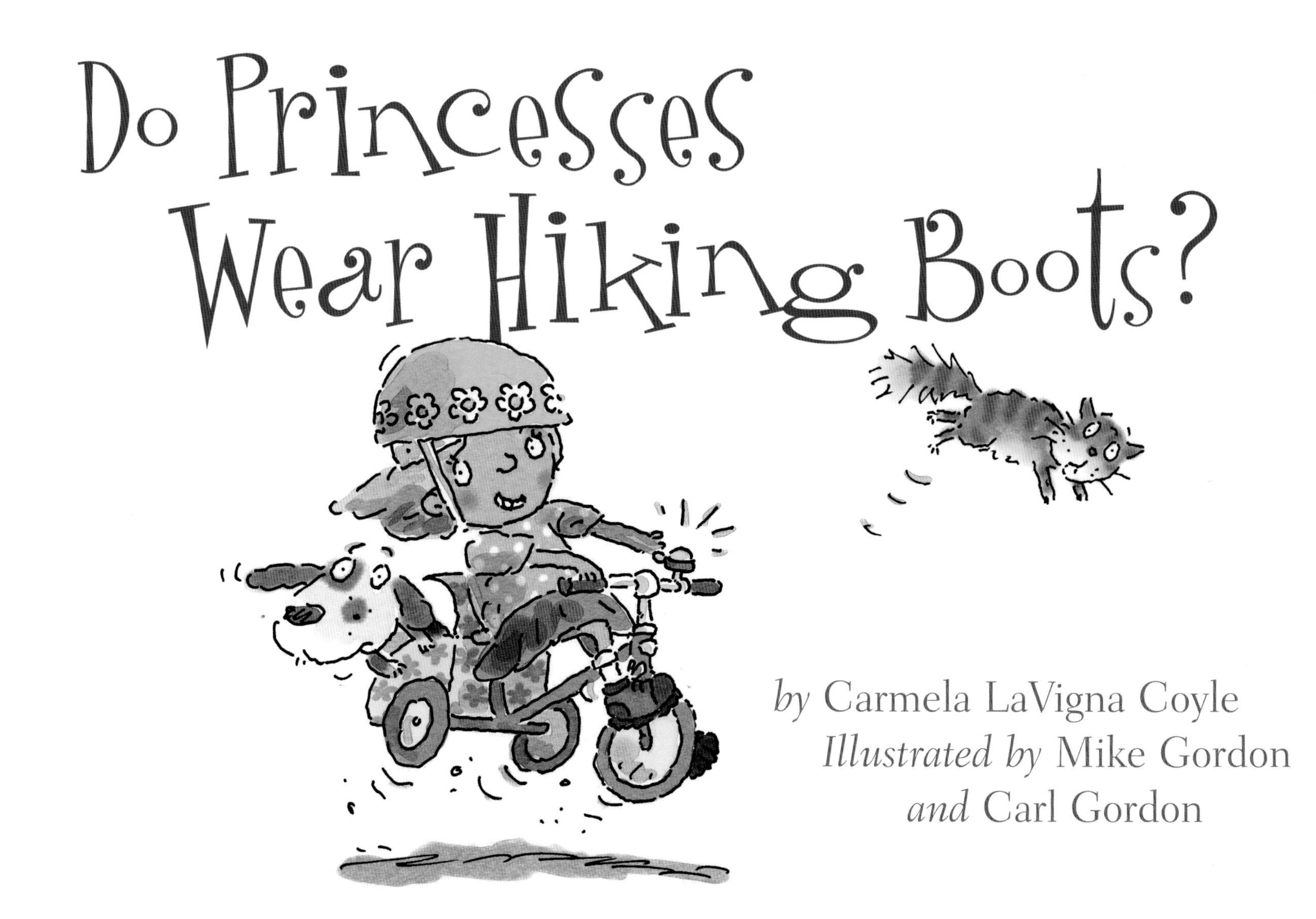

*by* Carmela LaVigna Coyle
*Illustrated by* Mike Gordon
*and* Carl Gordon

www.northlandpub.com

Composed in the United States of America
Printed in Yuanzhou, China September 2018
Text was set in Fairfield
Display text is set in Randumhouse

Edited by Theresa Howell
Designed by David Jenney
Production supervised by Donna Boyd

FIRST IMPRESSION 2003
ISBN 0-87358-828-2
ISBN 978-0-87358-828-7

Library of Congress Cataloging-in-Publication Data

Coyle, Carmela LaVigna
Do princesses wear hiking boots? / written by Carmela LaVigna Coyle ; illustrated by
Mike Gordon.
p. cm.
Summary: When a little girl asks her mother about princesses, she learns that they are
much like herself.
[1. Princesses—Fiction. 2. Self-perception—Fiction. 3. Mothers and daughters—Fiction.
4. Stories in rhyme.] I. Gordon, Mike, ill. II. Coyle, Carmela LaVigna III. Title.

PZ8.3C8396 Do 2003
[E]—dc21 2002031626

*To my darling Annie...for asking the question!*
*—clvc*

Mommy, do princesses wear hiking boots?

*When they wish to take the scenic routes.*

Do princesses ride tricycles?

*Yes, even two-wheel bicycles.*

Do princesses climb trees?

*Is there a better way to catch the breeze?*

Do princesses like to walk in the rain?

*They dance through the puddles without refrain!*

Do princesses play in the sand and dirt?

*If they're wearing jeans and a messy old shirt.*

Do princesses have to do any chores?

*They clean their drawers and sweep their floors.*

Mommy, do princesses have to follow the rules?

*That's one of the things they learn at school.*

Do princesses eat the crusts of their bread?

They save them for the ducks instead.

Do princesses have a favorite vegetable?

*They find them all delectable.*

Do princesses drink sparkling punch?

*They prefer lemonade with lunch.*

When princesses laugh, do they sometimes snort?

*They have manners of every sort.*

Do princesses cry and make a fuss?

They have bad hair days just like us.

Do princesses snore when they fall asleep?

*After they've counted 500 sheep.*

Mommy, do princesses seem at all like me?

*"A princess is
a place in your heart."*

*Look inside yourself and see…*